The
BIG
MONSTER
snoReYBOOK

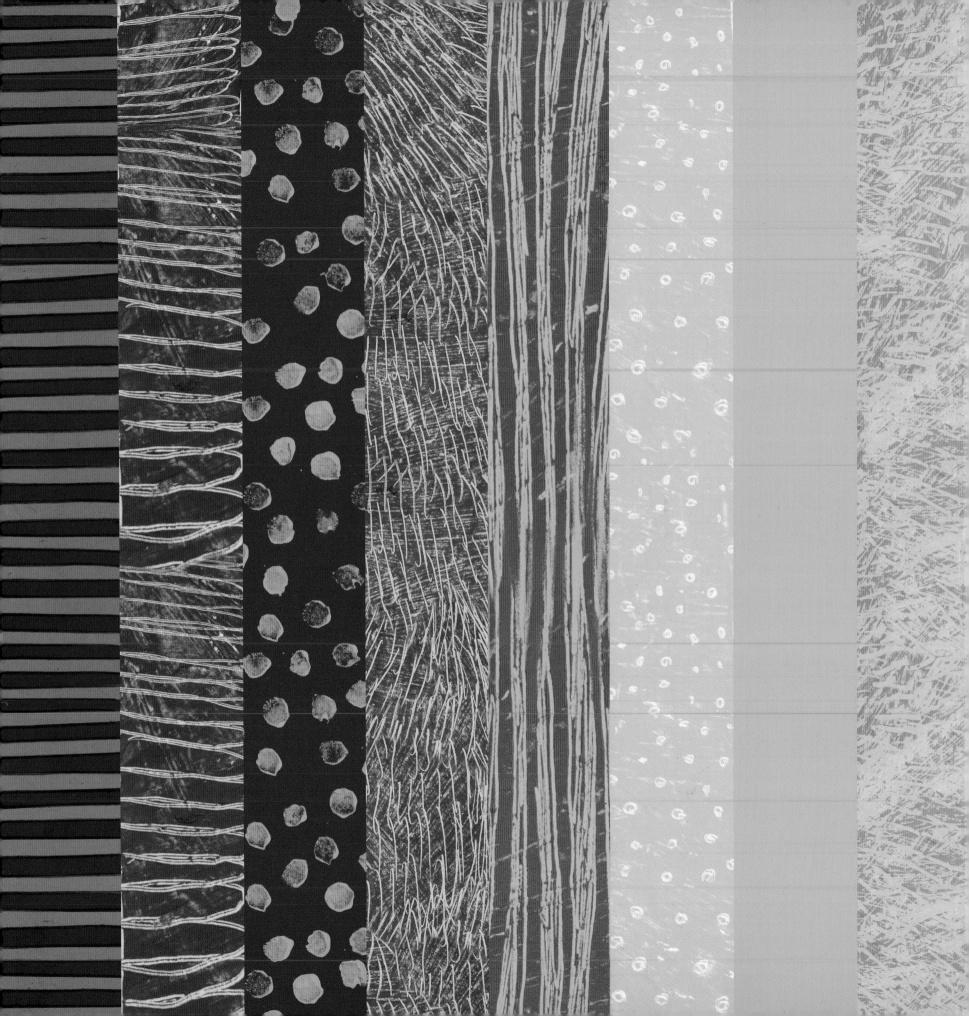

For my dear little Monster Sidney who prefers ALL to be WIDE AWAKE

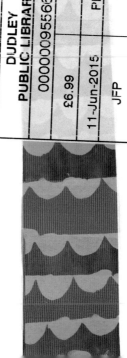

First published in 2015 by Nosy Crow Ltd. The Crow's Nest, 10a Lant Street, London SE1 1QR www.nosycrow.com

ISBN 978 0 85763 330 9 (HB) ISBN 978 0 85763 331 6 (PB)

Nosy Crow and associated logos are trademarks and/or registered trademarks of Nosy Crow Ltd.

Text and illustration copyright © Leigh Hodgkinson 2015
The right of Leigh Hodgkinson to be identified as the author and illustrator of this work has been asserted.

A CIP catalogue record for this book is available from the British Library.

Printed in China. Papers used by Nosy Crow are made from wood grown in sustainable forests.

1 3 5 7 9 8 6 4 2 (HB) 1 3 5 7 9 8 6 4 2 (PB)

The BIG MONSTER SnoReYBOOK

LEIGH HODGKINSON

SPECIAL DELIVERY

Little Monster

nosy crow

Oh dear. I am sorry to say that you happen to be reading a **very** dull book.

There is **NOTHING** to see here.

That's right . . .

. . . **NOTHING.**

Little Monster

HOW TO USE
PLAY
STOP
RECORD
HAVE FUN!

Testing, testing, 1, 2, 3.

You see, everyone is fast asleep.

(This is a snoreybook, after all.)

But it's **completely** up to you
if you want to carry on reading . . .

Shhh! Pretend you HAVEN'T seen me, ok?

. . . oh good, you have decided to give it a go then, have you?

Well, this is **norris.**

Unfortunately, Norris fell asleep as soon as you opened this book. Norris's knobbly knees knock while his tiny toothypegs chillily chatter.

Apart from that, there is **NOTHING** to see here.

ZZZZZZ JIBBER ZZZZZ JABBER ZZZZ

Before you opened this book,

I DO believe they were talking about YOU.

It's a shame you weren't reading this page then.

Never mind.

Apart from that, there is **NOTHING** to see here.

Here's **TONY.**

Tony's toes tippy tap while he dreams.

Perhaps tomorrow Tony might get around to
snipping those terribly
tatty toenails.

ZZZZZZZZZZZZZZZZZZZZ

TIPPY TAP TAP

I hope **YOU** haven't got big monster toenails.

When did you last check?

Apart from that, there is **NOTHING** to see here.

Gently does it...

This here is **FIONa.**

Fiona fussily fidgets and scritches
and scratches.

Look, Fiona's five, fluffy, flapping
feet are twizzled up into a knot.

If only you'd looked at this page a
moment ago – you'd have seen
Fiona **frantically** flip
onto her back.

ZZZZ

Ooh! I think
this will be
VERY useful.

THUD

THUMP

THUNK

ZZZZZZZzz

But you missed it, didn't you?
Apart from that, there is
NOTHING to see here.

SCRITCH

SCRATCH

Last of all it's **BRIAN.**

Brian has a super-sized sweet tooth. Brian's **BIG** belly burbles as he dreams of **monster** cream cakes.

If you happen to be **very** sweet, best make sure you are **nowhere** near Brian when he wakes up.

So, that's it – all the snorey monsters in this book. All most DEFINITELY asleep.

Hang about . . .
perhaps I was **wrong**
about this book!

Perhaps there **is**
something going on . . .

Digging
holes
sure is
tiring.

What a noisy alarm clock!

Now those **BIG** monsters

are all wide awake.

And after their monster size snooze

they are ALL VERY hungry . . .

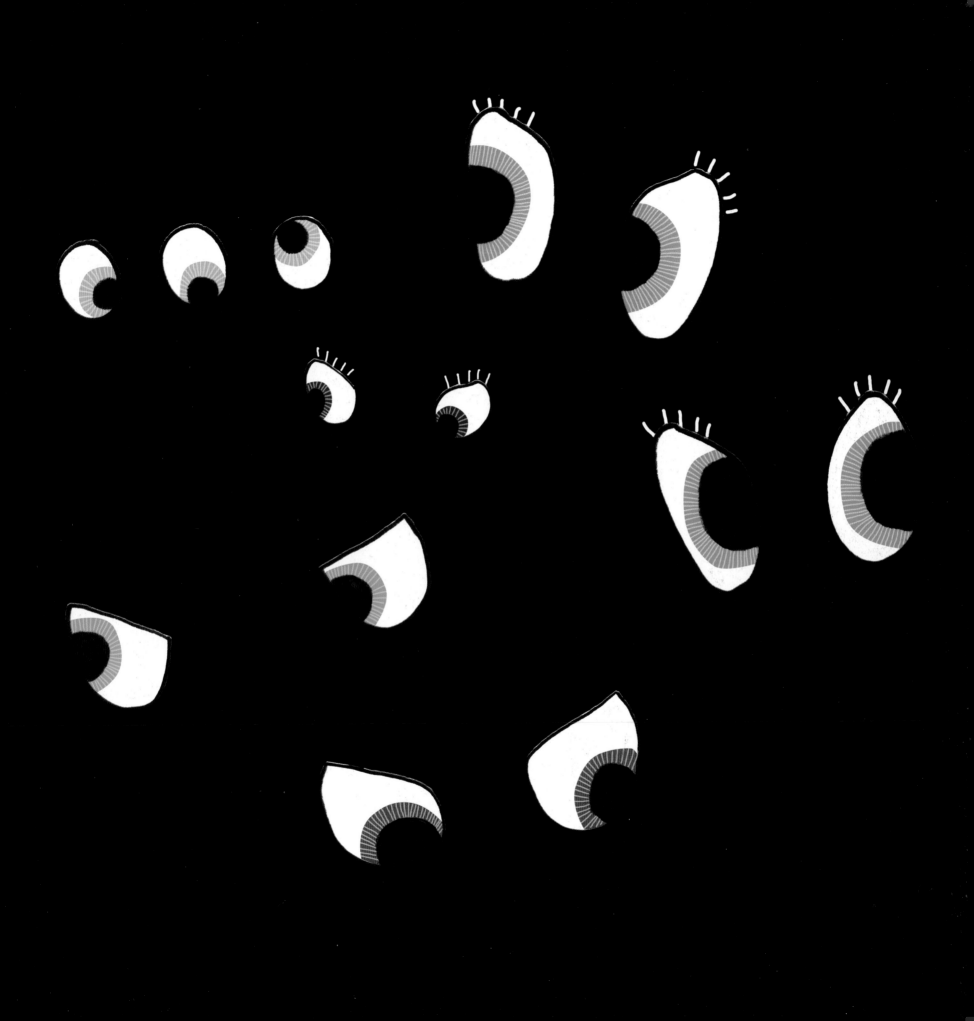

Luckily for you, **BIG** monsters don't like eating little children.

BIG monsters like eating little monsters. You didn't spot a little monster, did you?

What's all that NOISE? It couldn't be an even BIGGER monster, could it? What do you suppose an even BIGGER monster might like to eat?

Well, these BIG monsters sure aren't going to stick around to find out!

Hee hee! I LOVE it when a plan comes together!

Well, that's got rid of all those
BIG noisy monsters.

Let's all enjoy a little bit

of peace and quiet now, shall we?

Goodnight.